Take Care

[signature]

The Swetsville Zoo

by Kerry Davis

All sculptures by
Bill Swets, Zoo Creator and Owner

Thanks again to
Bronco Lee
who made this book possible.

Special thanks to:
Tim O'Hara Photography
John Robledo
Rod Stewart

Illustrated by Karen Large

To my wife
Tina
the real zookeeper

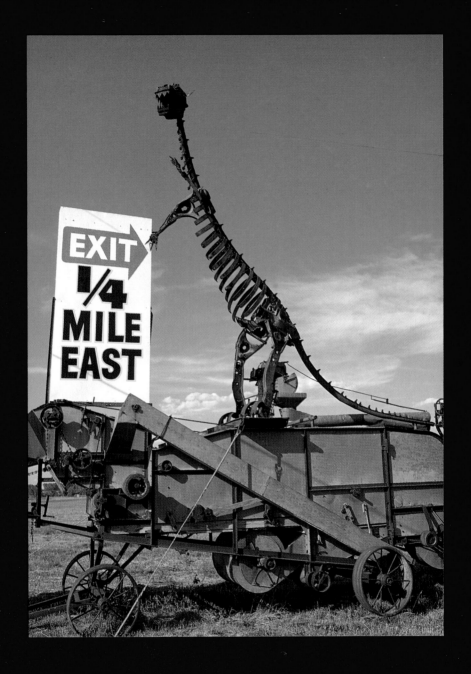

The sign read
turn right a quarter mile.
And when I turned
I began to smile.

This is a place
With unusual charm.
Down by the river
It's a funky farm.

The animals here
Are a motley crew,
Crazy critters at the
Swetsville Zoo.

They don't make noises

And they don't run.

They don't eat anything.

They're just for fun.

Replicas of a different age

And not one needs a cage.

There's creatures of old

And saurus of new

And I'm told
A lot of them flew.

Now Bill Swets owns this farm,
The land and the animals too.

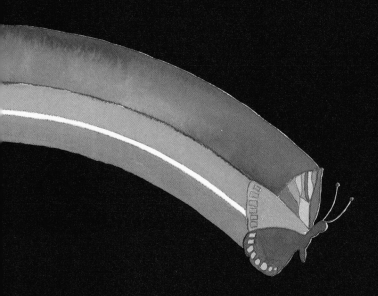

He created these creatures
And called it the Swetsville Zoo.

He takes old farm machinery,
A truck or a car
Welds and bends
Fastens and mends

And...

Here they are...

Here's some of the names
That Bill Swets chose.
Since he created these creatures
Bill Swets knows.

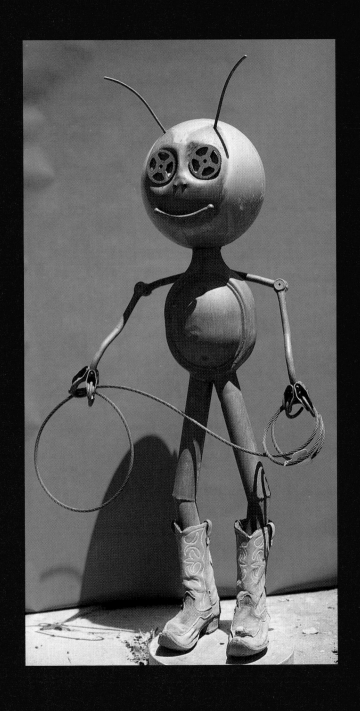

Marty the Martian Cowboy...
He's a cowboysaurus.

Gary the Gargoyle

If there were space creatures,

This is what they would look like.
Ricky, Vicky, Micky, Dicky and Tricky

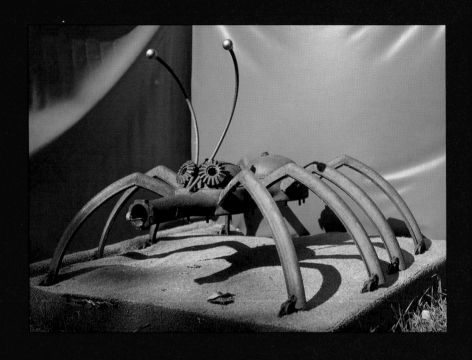

Snyder the Spider

Gee the Bee
Don't sting me!

Mr. Bad Wrench

Is getting a ticket from the

Autosaurus

What to drive!

He's a circus high wire act.
His balance has to be exact.

They used ancient oil
So their wheels wouldn't squeak
It looks like they need it
So their bones won't creak.

Harry the Hitchhiker

Little Toot

Sly the Fly and Jerry

You've got to dig for worms
Before you go fishing.

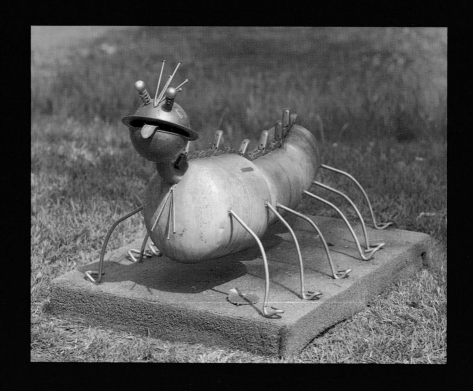

Conrad Caterpillar

Ernie Fixit
Looking for the Tin Man.

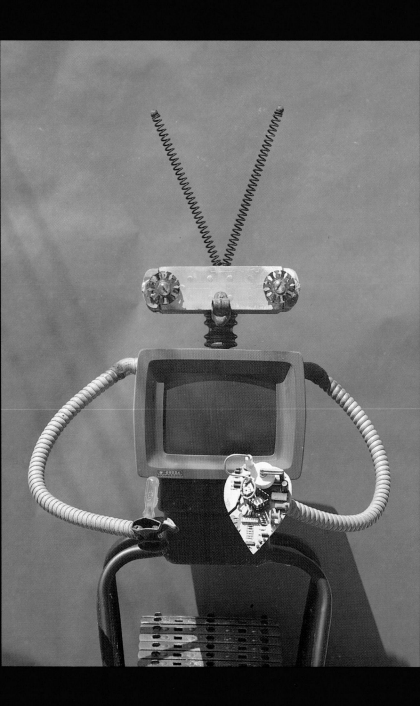

Huey, he's an electronics wiz.

They learned to play drums
On an old car trunk.
Now the music that
They play is heavy metal junk.

You name it!

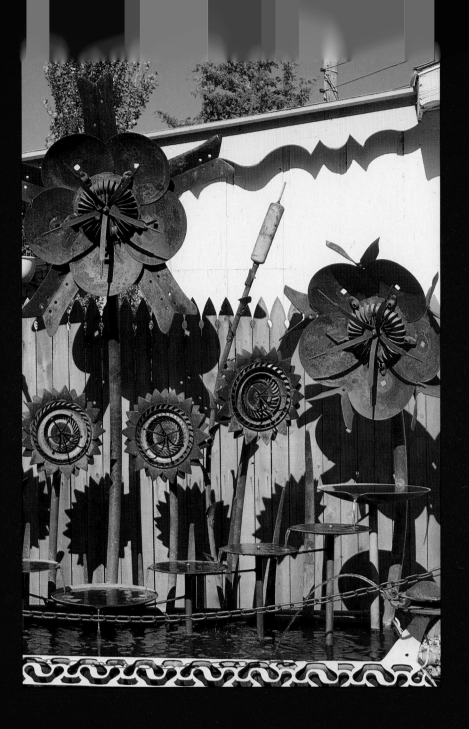

The zoo in full bloom.

Thanks for the thrill — Bill
Make some more,
Say you will.

We'll have to come back
In a season or two
And see what's new
At the Swetsville Zoo.

Be good 'til then
And we'll be seeing you.

The Swetsville Zoo
is located in Ft. Collins, Colorado,
just east of I-25, Exit 265.

Until you can come by and say "Hi,"
Don't forget to support
your local zoo!